W9-ALM-509

SOMETHING SLIMY
ON PRIMROSE DRIVE

by Karen Wallace
illustrated by Helen Flook

Librarian Reviewer
Kathleen Baxter
Children's Literature Consultant
formerly with Anoka County Library, MN
BA College of Saint Catherine, St. Paul, MN
MA in Library Science, University of Minnesota

Reading Consultant
Elizabeth Stedem
Educator/Consultant, Colorado Springs, CO
MA in Elementary Education, University of Denver, CO

STONE ARCH BOOKS
Minneapolis   San Diego

J
WAL

First published in the United States in 2007
by Stone Arch Books,
151 Good Counsel Drive, P.O. Box 669,
Mankato, Minnesota 56002.
www.stonearchbooks.com

Originally published in Great Britain in 2002
by A & C Black Publishers Ltd,
38 Soho Square, London, W1D 3HB.

Library of Congress Cataloging-in-Publication Data
Wallace, Karen.
    Something Slimy on Primrose Drive / by Karen Wallace; illustrated by
Helen Flook. — 1st U.S. ed.
    p. cm. — (Pathway Books)
    Summary: When the strange Wolfbane family moves in next to the
ultraconservative Rigid-Smythes, changes and misunderstandings flourish as
the families attempt to track down a notorious thief.
    ISBN-13: 978-1-59889-113-3 (hardcover)
    ISBN-10: 1-59889-113-8 (hardcover)
    ISBN-13: 978-1-59889-265-9 (paperback)
    ISBN-10: 1-59889-265-7 (paperback)
    [1. Neighbors—Fiction. 2. Individuality—Fiction. 3. Friendship—
Fiction.] I. Flook, Helen, ill. II. Title.
PZ7.W1568So 2007
[Fic]—dc22   2006005084

Art Director: Heather Kindseth
Graphic Designer: Kay Fraser

1 2 3 4 5 6 11 10 09 08 07 06

Table of Contents

CHAPTER 1

Primrose Drive was a nice, neat, tidy street where nice, neat, tidy people lived nice, neat, tidy lives.

Every house shined with new paint. Every flowerbed had rows of bright flowers. The grass was perfectly cut.

As for children on Primrose Drive, there were hardly any. Everyone said that children were too messy.

One night, the nice, neat, and tidy people of Primrose Drive were asleep when two black horses, pulling a huge, old carriage, trotted down the street at midnight.

It was a strange carriage. It had four creaky wheels and was loaded with what looked like coffins and hat boxes. It was covered in dripping scum and weeds. It looked as if it had been driven through a swamp at high speed. That's exactly what had happened. Boris Wolfbane liked going fast and the Wolfbanes' last home had been in a swamp.

Boris and Anaconda Wolfbane were anxious to make a good impression on their neighbors. Pearl and Clod were getting older, and Anaconda and Boris wanted them to have the kind of childhood they saw through windows on other people's TVs.

Primrose Drive was the perfect place.

* * * *

Inside the slimy black carriage, Anaconda wrapped up the leftovers of their picnic supper, chilled toadburgers with all the trimmings.

Anaconda sighed and gently patted Pearl's cheek.

"I wish you'd try a little bit of toadburger," she said. "It tastes just like chicken, you know."

"I know, Mom," replied Pearl Wolfbane kindly. She leaned back into the velvet seat. "But I'd rather eat chicken like everyone else."

At that moment, the carriage stopped.

"We're here!" cried Boris. Clod and Pearl scrambled out of their seats and jumped to the ground. Anaconda oozed out the door.

For a moment nobody spoke. Pearl stared so hard she thought her eyes might pop out.

In front of her was a perfectly ordinary house. Beside it was another perfectly ordinary house. Bright new paint gleamed in the moonlight. The grass looked like plastic. There was even a garage.

"Which one is ours?" whispered Pearl. She was so happy she could barely speak.

Boris Wolfbane spread his cloak and fluttered gently to the ground in front of No. 34.

Pearl hugged herself with joy. She had never seen such a lovely house. It was amazingly, unbelievably normal.

Clod Wolfbane turned to his sister and rolled his eyes. "Wow!" he whispered. "Is this weird or what?"

CHAPTER 2

The next morning, Anaconda Wolfbane tied on her favorite apron and handed out four bowls of green stew with gray lumps.

Anaconda was very excited. During the night, she and Boris had worked on the kitchen. Anaconda wanted to do everything she could to make Clod and Pearl feel completely at home for their first breakfast.

Boris had teased Anaconda and called her new kitchen a fancy cave.

Anaconda didn't mind. It wasn't a cave. It was an underground space with mud effects on the ceiling.

As for the water that ran down the walls, Anaconda had chosen a special color. It was burnt orange. Not at all the sort of thing you would find in a cave!

"More stew, dear?" asked Anaconda as Clod slurped up the last mouthful. Clod smiled and nodded.

"Pearl?" asked her mother.

"No thanks, Mom," replied Pearl. "I had some cereal and yogurt earlier."

"Yuck," said Clod. "That's disgusting!"

"Now, Clod," said Boris, as he picked his teeth with a chicken bone. "We all express ourselves in different ways." Boris put down his bone and a broad grin spread across his face.

"And speaking of expressing ourselves," he added. "Have you seen my new swimming pool?"

Pearl's pale round face lit up with delight. "Oh, Dad!" she cried. "I've always wanted a swimming pool. Now we can have parties and barbecues!"

Boris was rather pleased with himself. He, too, had noticed that swimming pools went very well with crowds, roasting meat, and getting to know people.

Clod was so excited that he swallowed the last gray lump of stew in one piece. "Can we see your pool, Dad?" he cried, choking and shouting at once.

"Of course," replied Boris proudly. "I've even put a few snakes in it to make it look prettier."

"I love swimming with snakes," cried Anaconda. "They're so friendly."

"Especially when they wrap themselves around your legs," said Clod.

Anaconda clapped her hands with delight. "That's a wonderful idea, darling! Let's have a dip!"

There was a screech of wooden stools against the rock floor. Suddenly Anaconda, Boris, and Clod were gone, and Pearl was left alone in the kitchen.

Pearl didn't really mind having a water hole crawling with snakes instead of a swimming pool. In a way, it would be more of a surprise if it was anything different. It was just that Pearl wished her family would do something that was the same as other people.

Pearl walked up the spiral stone stairs and pushed aside the thick hanging vines that were across the front door.

Just as she expected, where just last night there had been a perfect green lawn, she found herself looking at a mudhole full of water.

Pearl watched as her mother and brother splashed and played one of their favorite games. Clod swam as fast as he could and made a path through the scum. Then Anaconda had to catch him before the scum closed over the water again.

"What do you think?" cried Boris from an overhanging branch.

"It's brilliant, Dad," called Pearl in the most excited voice she could manage.

Splot! Boris dropped into the middle of the pond. "I knew you'd like it," he sputtered as he surfaced in the water.

Just then, Clod paddled toward them.

"Mom says we can do what we want with our bedrooms," he shouted to his sister. "She says I can have my scorpions and everything!"

"Of course you can, darling," said Anaconda. "We must all express our feelings in the things we surround ourselves with."

Boris carefully hauled himself out of the pond and sat on the edge where Pearl was standing.

Sunlight sparkled in Pearl's long, blonde hair. Her mouth was pink as a rosebud against her creamy skin.

Boris never tired of looking at his daughter. She was so pale and golden and beautiful. So completely different from the rest of her family.

"Have you thought how you'd like your bedroom, Pearl?" asked Boris.

Pearl sat down and held her father's hand. "Yes," she said. "I've thought about it a lot."

In fact, Pearl had thought about nothing else all those times in the past when she had stared at bedroom walls that were hollowed out of tree trunks or cut from rock or hung with seaweed or animal skins.

"My room is going to be pink and white," said Pearl firmly. "I want wallpaper with ribbons and flowers on it, teddy bears on my bed, and a dressing table with lace."

For a second, nobody spoke.

Then a large bubble went *pop!* as Anaconda's head sank beneath the scum.

CHAPTER 3

The Wolfbanes weren't the only family to arrive on Primrose Drive at midnight.

A few days later, the Rigid-Smythes drove toward Primrose Drive in their new, silver car. Pamela and Dudley with their two children, Simon and Ruby, were coming home from their vacation.

The Rigid-Smythes didn't usually travel at midnight. In this case, their late arrival was due to their plane being delayed.

Pamela was angry because she had made a special supper and put it in the freezer. She had dated it and stacked it so it would be easy to find on their first night back. She didn't like sudden changes.

Dudley Rigid-Smythe was angry, too. He was supposed to play a very important game of golf the next morning, with a business partner named Sid Bouncer.

Dudley had met Sid at the golf club a couple of months ago. Sid was smart at business and was a man of the world, like Dudley was.

Sid had suggested that they should buy the empty house next to Dudley's, No. 34 Primrose Drive. They'd split it into apartments and sell them for lots of money. All Dudley had to do was come up with half of the money.

At first, Dudley was nervous.

The only cash he had was in a savings account for Ruby and Simon. But Sid had explained that a good businessman has to take risks in order to make lots of money. If you play things safe all your life, you will never be a millionaire.

Dudley wanted to be a millionaire more than anything else in the whole, wide world. He was sure that if he were a millionaire, people would notice him.

In the back seat of the new car, Simon Rigid-Smythe fell into a light sleep. He didn't care what time he got home as long as he could start wearing lots of clothes again. Every morning for the past two weeks, he had been forced to listen to his mother moan how skinny he looked in his swimming trunks. How he should take better care of himself. Eat healthy food. Play on the beach with the other boys.

Simon wore a bathrobe into the water. He told his mother he was protecting himself from the sun.

Next to Simon, his sister, Ruby, stared into the night. Ruby loved everything to do with the night, especially staring into a full moon. Especially at midnight.

At that moment, a cloud turned itself into a dragon. "Mom!" cried Ruby. "There's a dragon flying across the moon!"

But when Pamela looked, all she saw was a moon with cloudy shadows across it. She turned and glared at her daughter. "How many times do I have to tell you? Stop making up stories."

"Now, now, Pamela," said Dudley. "We've had a nice, long vacation. We're all tired. Ruby was only imagining things."

"I wasn't imagining anything," said Ruby. "I saw a dragon."

Dudley ignored his daughter. "Anyway, in five minutes, we'll all be sleeping in our beds," he said.

Pamela sighed. She didn't mean to be so upset with Ruby, but she wished her daughter could be like other girls.

For the past two weeks, she had tried everything to get Ruby to join in with the other families on the beach. After all, there were lots of girls her age to play with. There were dances to go to and a shopping mall nearby. But Ruby didn't like dances and she hated shopping.

So while all the other girls twirled or tried on clothes, Ruby sat by herself staring into a rock pool.

The car filled with a thick silence as Dudley turned onto Primrose Drive.

"Almost home," he said. The words froze on his lips. In the bright beam of the car's headlights, the two houses were as clear and sharp as cardboard cutouts. The Rigid-Smythe's house, No. 33, was exactly as they had left it. The problem was the house next door.

This house looked like the set for a horror movie. A crooked tower stuck out of the roof. Where the front lawn had once been there was a dark forest of overgrown trees.

Something was terribly wrong. Pamela moaned, shook her head twice, and then didn't move again. It was as if she was stuck to the front seat.

A minute later, Dudley got out of the car and lifted his golf bag down from the roof. Now his game of golf with Sid Bouncer was more important than ever.

Simon and Pearl jumped out of the car.
They stood and looked up at the house
next to theirs. Simon's mouth was a great
big O. Ruby's mouth had turned into a
huge grin.

Hidden behind the railings of No. 34,
Anaconda and Boris watched their new
neighbors arrive.

"Boris," whispered Anaconda. "Look at
that fabulous snake carrier!" In the dark
night, Anaconda's eyes glowed like purple
flames. "Everything is going to be perfect,
Boris," she cried happily. "I just know it!"

CHAPTER 4

Pearl Wolfbane lay on her princess bed. The early morning sun shined through the pink curtains at her window. She swung out of bed and dug her toes into the thick carpet that covered the floor. She crossed the room to open her curtains.

Pearl's room was at the front of the house. Ever since she had arrived at Primrose Drive, she got up early in the morning, opened her window, and leaned out to gaze down the road at the gardens.

Pearl sighed happily. Everything about her new house was perfect.

There was only one thing that Pearl missed in her new house. She hadn't seen any other kids on Primrose Drive.

At that moment, Pearl turned to look at the house next door. She was expecting it to be empty as usual. It wasn't.

Pearl saw a bicycle lying on its side in the road. It was exactly the model Pearl had asked for at her last birthday. It had shiny silver handlebars, a white leather seat, and matching saddlebags.

Pearl looked over the jungle of trees and bushes that Anaconda had planted at the front gate. The bike she had actually been given was leaning against their white picket fence. It was a black, rusty, three-wheeler that made a terrible creaking noise when you rode it.

Of course, Anaconda and Boris had been delighted with Pearl's present. They had searched every junk shop until they found the perfect thing.

At that moment, Pearl heard a loud creak! Only one thing made that noise! Her own rusty three-wheeler! A girl Pearl's age was standing beside Pearl's bike. She had a face the color of chalk and her thick, black hair was cut in a crooked hairstyle.

The girl was staring at Pearl's bike. She looked as if she wanted the rusty old bike more than anything else in the world.

Pearl ran to Clod's bedroom.

"Clod!" she shouted. "Wake up!"

High above her in a hammock hanging from the rafters, Clod Wolfbane grunted and stirred.

There was no wallpaper in Clod's
room. There wasn't even any plasterboard
on the walls. Clod had stripped everything
down to the bare brick and floorboards.
Then he had made shelves out of boards
and concrete blocks. They were stuffed
with metal cages. Each cage contained a
spider, a shiny scorpion, or a lizard.

Underneath Clod's hammock was a trampoline, which he used instead of a ladder to get up to bed. Pearl climbed onto it and began to bounce.

Four bounces later, she poked the lump in the hammock that was her brother.

"Clod! Get up! We've got neighbors!"

Clod sat up. "Neighbors?" he shouted. "Why didn't you say so?"

As Pearl hopped off the trampoline, Clod rolled out of his hammock. Then he bounced and landed in front of his sister.

Ten minutes later, Clod and Pearl were climbing through the thick branches of an oak tree that separated the two gardens.

"Are you sure this is a good idea?" muttered Pearl. "What happens if they see us spying on them? They might think we're weird."

Clod chuckled. "So what? Who cares? It doesn't matter."

But it did matter to Pearl. She decided to take a quick peek, then go around and introduce herself like normal people do.

At that moment, Pearl pushed through a cluster of leaves and for the first time she saw their new neighbors' back garden.

Pearl couldn't believe her eyes! At the end of a beautiful lawn, with flower beds on either side, was a sparkling blue swimming pool. "Wow!" cried Pearl. "What a fantastic swimming pool!"

"If you like that sort of thing."

Pearl froze. The voice was deep and scratchy. It didn't sound like Clod at all. Pearl felt every hair on the back of her neck stand up. She turned and found herself staring into the chalky face of the girl she had seen from her window.

"I like your water hole much better," said the girl. Her black eyes sparkled. "And I think your bike is cool."

Pearl was so surprised that she said the first thing that came into her head. "I always wanted a bike like yours and I think your swimming pool is cool!"

For a moment neither girl spoke.

Then they both burst out laughing.

"My name's Ruby," said the dark-haired girl. She didn't sound angry anymore. "Ruby Rigid-Smythe."

"I'm Pearl Wolfbane," said Pearl.

Clod's head dropped between them. He was hanging upside down from a branch above. "Hi. I'm Clod, Pearl's brother."

Ruby laughed. "I've got a brother too," she said. "His name is Simon."

"Cool!" cried Clod. He dropped down beside his sister. "Where is he?"

Ruby shrugged. "Asleep, I guess."

Clod grinned. "Why don't you wake him up and I'll cook toadburgers for breakfast?"

Pearl went bright red.

"Clod!" she cried. "How can you talk about toadburgers? You'll make Ruby feel sick."

"It's okay," said Ruby. "I've heard of toadburgers. They're like chicken but better!" She laughed. "Simon will eat anything!"

"Okay," said Pearl. "We'll have a breakfast picnic in our tree house!"

"Anything you say," said Clod. "I'll go get everything ready." He climbed down through the branches and disappeared.

Pearl was expecting Ruby to go too,
but Ruby didn't move. Instead she sat and
pulled apart a leaf in her hand.

Suddenly Pearl's stomach was full of
butterflies. Maybe she'd said something
wrong. Maybe Ruby didn't want to have
a picnic breakfast after all. Pearl bit her
lip. She was so looking forward to having
friends next door.

"It doesn't matter if Simon doesn't like toadburgers," said Pearl. She shrugged. "I mean, I don't."

Ruby looked into Pearl's clear blue eyes. "I wasn't even thinking about toadburgers," she said. "I was thinking about your tree house. We've always wanted a tree house."

"Tree houses are easy to build," cried Pearl. "You should just ask your dad to put up the frame."

Ruby ripped up her leaf and watched it fall to the ground. "We've asked our dad hundreds of times," she said. "He always says no."

For some reason that Pearl didn't quite understand, she put out her hand and patted Ruby's arm. "It's okay if you don't have your own tree house," she said gently. "You and Simon can share ours."

CHAPTER 5

Simon Rigid-Smythe watched the morning sun climb into the sky. He looked at his watch. He had another forty-five minutes before his mother knocked on his door to wake him up.

Slowly, without making any noise, Simon opened his closet and dragged a trunk into the middle of the room. He took a key from around his neck and opened the lid.

There were two sections in the trunk.

One was packed with screwdrivers, pliers, hammers, wires, batteries, and all kinds of motor parts.

The other side was stacked with tiny working robots, made to do anything Simon wanted them to do. Some picked up pieces of paper and fuzz from under his bed. Others sharpened his pencils. One polished his shoes. And one did nothing but find missing socks.

Simon grinned to himself and picked up the robot he was working on. The truth was that Simon Rigid-Smythe was a genius. And the only one who knew it was his sister Ruby.

At that moment, there were two sharp taps on the door. It was Ruby's signal. Simon replied with a low whistle and Ruby came into the room. Her face was red and excited.

"Hurry up!" she whispered. "We've been invited to a breakfast picnic in a tree house!"

Simon opened his mouth to speak but Ruby pointed toward their parents' bedroom. Simon nodded. She didn't have to explain. They had to get out fast before their parents woke up and found a reason to say no.

* * * *

"A picnic breakfast!" said Anaconda over and over. "What a wonderful idea!" In front of her a large basket was packed with toadburgers, fruit, crunchy chocolate beetles, sugar snakes, and a huge watermelon.

"Ruby went to get Simon," cried Pearl in a high, excited voice. "She's really nice, Mom. I'm so glad they live next door."

Boris looked up from the newspaper he was reading as he hung upside down from the ceiling.

He believed that the longer you hung upside down, the smarter you became. "I knew you'd make friends," he said.

"Everything's ready!" Clod's face appeared at the door. "I'll be out at the tree house!"

Pearl picked up the basket and ran up the stone stairs into the sunlight.

"Oh, Boris," cried Anaconda. "I'm so excited! Our first new neighbors!"

Boris's face was now almost purple. "Anaconda!" he cried. "I've just had the best idea." He flipped backward and landed on the stone floor. "Let's invite our new neighbors to a meat roast by the mud hole!" He took his wife in his arms. "That's what other people do!"

"Oh, Boris!" cried Anaconda as they danced around the room. "I believe it is!"

* * *

Ruby had climbed up the rope ladder, but Simon was frozen to the spot. Because Simon wasn't the only one who collected broken bits and pieces. Clod collected things, too. And he kept them in a pile underneath the tree house.

So far Clod had three rusty lawn mowers, a couple of broken cars, a set of race car wheels, an old engine, and several steel rails and iron bars. "Wow!" Simon kept saying to himself. "Wow!"

Clod was hiding in the leaves watching him. Even though he looked and acted tough, the truth was that Clod was shy. Ruby and Pearl were friends, so Clod hoped that he and Simon could be, too.

When he had first seen Simon, he had been worried. Simon looked pale and thin and he moved as slowly as a stick insect. Clod spent most of his time crashing around like a pinball in an arcade machine. How could they be friends?

But as Clod watched Simon's face he knew he had nothing to worry about. Clod watched Simon staring at the junk on the ground and realized that Simon noticed everything.

Clod grabbed a vine and swung down to the grass. "I'm Clod," he said, holding out his hand.

"I'm Simon," said Simon. He shook Clod's hand. "Is this your junk?"

"Yup," said Clod.

A big smile spread across Simon's face. "Ever thought of building an airplane?"

CHAPTER 6

Pamela Rigid-Smythe groaned under her eye mask and moved the ice pack on her forehead. She had never had such awful nightmares. All night she had tossed and turned.

It was always the same terrible dream. They had come back from their vacation and found the house next door looking like a set from a horror movie.

"Dudley," she croaked. "Headache. Weak tea. Headache. Weak tea."

She reached out a pale arm to nudge her husband awake. But there was no one there! Pamela sat up and ripped the mask from her eyes. "Dudley!" she screamed. "Where are you?"

Dudley appeared from inside their walk-in closet. He was dressed in his golf clothes. In his right hand, he held his new golfing gloves. "Dudley!" shouted Pamela. "You can't leave me!"

Dudley's hand shook as he poured two cups of weak tea from the teapot on the bedside table. That morning, he had woken early and had decided to take a look at the house next door. It was possible that they had just been seeing things.

The house Dudley looked at was straight out of a Dracula movie. It made him feel sick to look at it.

And the more Dudley looked at it, the sicker he felt.

In Dudley's mind, he and Sid already owned No. 34. In fact, they had already turned it into apartments and he was already a millionaire. Now everything was ruined!

Pamela gulped her tea like a rabbit sucking from a water tube.

"I had horrible dreams about the house next door," she whispered.

Dudley Rigid-Smythe touched his wife's arm. "They weren't dreams," he whispered in a shaking voice. "That's why I'm playing golf with Sid Bouncer."

Pamela looked at her husband. He sounded like a madman.

"The reason I have to meet Sid Bouncer," said Dudley as if he was trying not to shout, "is because Sid Bouncer knows everyone. He is a powerful man."

Pamela groaned. She could feel a dull pain in her head.

"Sid Bouncer will know what to do," said Dudley. "He'll know the right person in the mayor's office. That person will convince these people to leave. Then everything will go just as I planned."

Pictures from her dream flashed through Pamela's mind. A crooked tower, a tangled jungle, a giant mudhole.

"So it's all true?" she croaked. Without another word, Pamela sank back and pulled the sheet over her head.

* * *

On the other side of town, in a trailer next to a used-car lot, Sid Bouncer was also getting ready for his game of golf with Dudley Rigid-Smythe.

Sid had things on his mind, too. But they were very different from Dudley's. Sid twisted a tie neatly around his neck and fixed it in place with a diamond pin.

Of the many things Sid knew, one of the most important was to look the part. Today Sid had to look perfect, because he was playing a very important part.

Next to him a woman in a gold
dressing gown stretched out her long legs
(even though there wasn't a lot of room
in the trailer) and then began to paint her
toenails red.

"Do you think he'll go for it, Sid?" asked
Goldie Bouncer. "Dudley might not be as
dumb as he looks."

"Of course he'll go for it," said Sid. "He thinks he's a clever businessman."

Sid slipped on a pair of expensive golf shoes that he had stolen from someone else's locker at the golf club the week before. Then he checked out his reflection in the mirror. He looked like a warthog with slick, black hair.

"If we're really lucky," Sid added, "he'll be dumb enough to have the money in a safe in his house."

Goldie stood up. "I'm good at finding safes," she said. A nasty grin spread across her face. "Why don't we meet Dudley and his wife for dinner?"

Sid smiled and kissed his wife on her forehead. "Anything you say, sweetest."

Sid and Goldie Bouncer were a team. They always worked in the same way.

First, Sid would join a golf club in a new area and look for a fool.

Then, Goldie would appear and talk to the fool's wife. Soon the two couples would be the best of friends.

That was the moment that Sid would come up with a business deal that would make them both millionaires.

It was always the same sort of scam. Buying a house and turning it into apartments. This time, the scam was so easy because the house Sid had suggested was the house next door to Dudley.

Goldie handed Sid a pair of new, golfing gloves she had stolen last week.

"Make sure you let him win," she said. "It will make him think that he's smarter than you."

CHAPTER 7

Three hours later, Sid leaned back on a lawn chair in the Rigid-Smythes' garden.

"You worry too much, Dudley," said Sid. "Your neighbors are doing us a favor. The place will be even cheaper once they leave."

"But how do you know they'll go?" asked Pamela.

Goldie smiled and patted Pamela's hand. "Don't you worry, dear," she said. "Sid takes care of these things."

"I certainly do," agreed Sid. "Leave it to me."

For the first time since they had come back from their vacation, Dudley Rigid-Smythe was beginning to feel better. Not only had he beaten Sid at golf, it also seemed that his plans weren't ruined after all. Dudley knew his part of the deal was ready. The money was packed in a briefcase in the safe inside his house.

"Mom. Dad. This is Pearl. She's our new neighbor."

All four adults froze. Pamela almost dropped the glass she was holding.

Ruby was standing next to a little girl. She had blonde hair and clear blue eyes and her clothes were neat and tidy. She didn't look at all like the kind of girl who would live in a crumbling castle and swim in a mud hole.

It wasn't the difference between the two girls that startled Pamela. It was the look on Ruby's face.

For the first time, Ruby looked happy.

"How lovely to meet you, Pearl," said Pamela quickly. "This is Dudley, Ruby's father, and Sid and Goldie Bouncer."

"Hello." Pearl smiled and her blue eyes sparkled. "We've been hoping we'd have neighbors ever since we arrived."

"What have you two been up to all day?" asked Pamela, who just realized she hadn't seen her daughter for hours.

"We've had an amazing time, Mom," cried Ruby. "First we had breakfast in Clod and Pearl's tree house, then we went out on our bikes." She laughed. "And we traded because I like Pearl's bike better than mine!"

Dudley smiled and ruffled his daughter's black hair. "I suppose it's this year's new model."

"Oh, no!" Ruby shook her head. "It's an old black three-wheeler with an amazing creak. Pearl's parents searched junk shops for it. And Pearl's mom wears these fantastic black dresses," cried Ruby. "And her dad hangs upside down in the kitchen like a bat!" Pearl's blush turned from pink to red. "And Simon and Clod are making something top secret!"

"Simon?" said Pamela. "I thought he was still asleep."

"Who's Clod?" asked Dudley.

"Sounds like a lump of dirt to me," said Goldie.

"Clod is Pearl's brother," replied Ruby, coldly. She didn't like Goldie. "He's got a cool junk collection."

She paused and looked at her mother. "And Simon really likes him."

Poor Pearl. She wished the ground would open and swallow her up. "I'd better go home now," she whispered to Ruby.

"What?" Ruby almost shouted. "But Pearl, I was going to show you my room."

Dudley forced a smile onto his face. Sid Bouncer winked at him. "Of course you must see Ruby's room, Pearl," said Dudley smoothly. "She's very proud of it."

Pamela took her cue from her husband. She turned to Pearl with a sweet smile. "And I'm sure Clod would like to come over with Simon."

"Simon likes it at Clod's house, Mom," said Ruby. Before Pamela could reply, Ruby took Pearl by the arm and led her into the kitchen.

At first Pearl couldn't believe what she was looking at. She had never seen a kitchen like this. All the cupboards and drawers were hidden. Even the sink was hidden under a sliding counter. There was no sign of food.

Pearl followed Ruby into the hall. Through the open doors, Pearl could see every room had the same sort of feel as the kitchen. Suddenly she realized that all the things she took for granted were missing. There were no paintings or books. There were no bunches of flowers. There was no clutter at all. It was as if no one lived there.

Then Pearl saw something that looked like a large, gold grate halfway up the wall. It was different from everything else and the only thing that looked as if the Rigid-Smythes had chosen it themselves. Pearl stopped. "What's that?"

Ruby made a face. "It's a safe." She walked over to the wall, pushed what looked like a light switch, and the gold grate swung open.

A sly smile appeared on Ruby's face. She went to the safe and turned the knob backward and forward. Soon, there was a loud click and the door opened.

"Ruby!" gasped Pearl. "You shouldn't!"

Ruby peered inside. "Nothing but a boring old briefcase," she said. She shut the safe door and pushed the grate back against the wall. At the window, a curtain fluttered. There was no wind that day. It was Goldie Bouncer's hand shaking with excitement.

A minute later, Pearl stood in the middle of Ruby's room trying to think of something to say. The walls and the ceilings were painted black and covered in fish. Some floated in midair, attached to strings from the ceiling. It was as if they were a thousand feet beneath the surface of the ocean. Pearl realized that her room must have seemed as weird to Ruby as Ruby's room seemed to her.

"So," said Ruby, "what do you think?"

Pearl turned to Ruby. "Amazing," she said, "but—"

"But what?"

Pearl felt confused. "It's so different from everything I've seen in your house."

"That's because my parents are weird."

"What!" Pearl couldn't believe her ears. "My parents are weird, not yours."

Ruby threw herself down on a chair. "Your parents are weird in a good way." Ruby's eyes looked angry and dark. "They don't mind if people are different from them. All my parents care about is being the same or better than everyone else."

Pearl thought of Boris and Anaconda. They didn't care if people did things in different ways. All they wanted was for everyone to be happy. "So your parents wouldn't like my parents."

Ruby nodded. "The truth is, they're probably frightened of your parents, even though they haven't met them!"

CHAPTER 8

"Crave!" said Anaconda. "That's a good word." She picked up a pen and began writing across a new sheet of paper.

"We crave your company for dinner." Anaconda looked up. "What do you think, Boris?"

Boris swung from the ceiling. "No," he said. "I don't think crave is right at all."

"I give up!" Anaconda scrunched up the paper into a ball and threw it on the floor. "You do it!" cried Anaconda.

"Do what?" asked Clod.

Anaconda spun around. Boris flipped backward and landed neatly on the floor. Clod was standing beside a pale, thin boy with red hair.

At first Anaconda thought the boy must be sick, because he was so pale. Then she noticed his eyes.

They sparkled like emeralds. It was as if they were lit up by a light bulb inside his head.

"This is Simon," said Clod. "He lives next door."

Simon smiled shyly. "Hello."

Anaconda bounded across the room. "Simon!" she cried. "How wonderful that you are here in my kitchen just when I have made something truly delicious, which I think you will really like!"

"Good to see you, Simon," said Boris. "Please sit down and join us."

Five minutes, later Simon was munching cake and sipping Boris's homemade chameleon punch.

"It's not made of real chameleons," Boris said.

"I call it chameleon punch because it changes color when you think different thoughts. Just one of my little experiments."

Simon was amazed. He felt comfortable with Clod's parents. He began to tell them all about his robots.

"Simon's a genius," said Clod.

His punch turned sky blue. "We're building an — oops! It's a secret."

"Only until it's ready," said Simon. His drink turned silver with red stripes. "Then everyone will know."

"How exciting," cried Anaconda. "I love secrets!"

"Why?" asked Simon.

"Because secrets can turn into wonderful surprises!" said Anaconda happily.

Then she had an idea. "Would your parents like to come to a surprise celebration?"

Simon almost choked on his cake. He suddenly remembered he hadn't seen them all day. Simon didn't know what to say. It was as if the mention of his parents had broken a magical spell.

"That settles it," cried Anaconda. "I'll invite them!" She picked up a pen and began to scratch a note.

Come to a surprise supper!

your new neighbors,

Boris and Anaconda Wolfbane.

Anaconda waved her arms around. "Would they prefer to eat in the dining area or outside by the roasted meat pit?"

Boris remembered what he'd read about getting to know people.

"Let's eat outside," he cried. "Then we can all have a dip in the mudhole!"

* * *

That was why, later that afternoon, Pamela and Dudley crept through a leafy green tunnel up to the Wolfbanes' front door. Ruby and Simon had gone over earlier. They both wanted to be with their neighbors as much as possible.

As Pamela brushed a leaf from her cheek, she couldn't help thinking about Simon when he had come home carrying the Wolfbanes' invitation. His face had looked shiny and pink, not dull and white. Somehow he even seemed to have grown and filled out.

As for Ruby, Pamela was still stunned by the change in her daughter.

She couldn't remember the last time Ruby had smiled, let alone laughed.

Now there was a brightness about her that Pamela had never seen before.

For the first time, tiny doubts began to bother Pamela. What right did she and Dudley have to stick their noses in the lives of a family that was different from theirs? They didn't need the money.

Pamela forced herself to face the truth. It was greed and fear that was behind their plan to make apartments. Suddenly Pamela's doubts turned into a cold, sick feeling in her stomach. What if Ruby and Simon found out that their own parents were planning to get rid of their friends and neighbors?

Pamela groaned. "They would never forgive us!" she said out loud.

Dudley turned to her. "What?" He had been lost in his own thoughts, thinking the same thing as Pamela.

"Nothing," said Pamela.

"Greetings, neighbors!" cried Boris.

Pamela and Dudley found themselves looking at a long, smiling face with eyes that glowed like coals. "Boris Wolfbane! At your service!"

He grasped Dudley's hand. It felt as firm as a wet fish. "Dudley Rigid-Smythe," said Dudley. "This is Pamela, my wife."

Boris took Pamela's cool, skinny hand in his. "Delighted," cried Boris. "Follow me! Anaconda awaits us!"

Pamela and Dudley followed Boris down the hallway. Even though No. 34 Primrose Drive was roughly the same size as No. 33, the hallway was more like a castle hall. Through open doors, they could see huge rooms hung with paintings and full of dark furniture.

"We made a few little changes when we arrived," Boris said. "Makes it seem more comfy, don't you think?"

Dudley looked up. Many of the floorboards had been taken away. Rafters crossed the house like ribs. "Much faster than using the stairs," explained Boris.

At that moment Anaconda entered from
what looked like a cave in the ground.
She was holding a silver tray with four tall
glasses. Behind her Pearl and Ruby were
giggling and chatting as they carried up
plates of tiny cakes.

Simon and Clod joked and laughed as they carried a huge crystal bowl filled with punch up the stairs.

Pamela was surprised by the change in her children. She wondered if Dudley had noticed it, too. Dudley was staring at a large, yellow frog swimming across the green, scummy water in the mud hole in front of them.

Anaconda put down her tray and shook Pamela's hand.

"We're so pleased to meet you," she cried. "Ruby and Simon have told us so much about you!" She smiled a sparkling smile at Dudley. "I knew from the moment I saw your clever snake carrier that we would get along!"

"I beg your pardon?" said Dudley.

Ruby laughed. "Mrs. Wolfbane means your golf club bag, Dad," she explained.

"Of course I do!" Anaconda poured out the shiny liquid into four glasses.

"It's a very old family recipe," she explained as Dudley and Pamela looked suspiciously at the glasses in their hands. "It's for celebrations."

Anaconda flashed her sparkling smile and raised her glass. "To wonderful things happening!"

"Truly wonderful things," added Boris.

"Uh, yes," said Dudley. He drained his glass to hide his embarrassment.

Anaconda immediately refilled it. "Now, tell me about this golf," she asked sweetly. "Do you play it with snakes?"

Pamela made a sound like a camel choking and finished her drink.

Boris smiled and refilled it.

Anaconda thought hard. What sort of thing would fit into a long, thin bag? "Or do you use bones?" she asked.

Ruby and Simon exchanged worried looks with Pearl and Clod. They wanted so much for their parents to get along.

Clod had secretly raided Boris's private cupboard, found half a bottle of Get Along Gumption at the back, and poured it into the punch. Things weren't going well at all. Maybe the Get Along Gumption had gone stale.

"What are we going to do?" whispered Ruby helplessly. Then Simon had an idea. If there was one thing his father couldn't resist, it was showing off his golf swing.

"I'll set up the practice net and bring over the clubs," he shouted. "Dad can show Mrs. Wolfbane how to swing."

Anaconda clapped her hands.

Everything was going so smoothly. It was lovely having neighbors. "What a clever idea, Simon!" she cried.

Then something odd happened. Dudley burst out laughing. "I'd be delighted to show you my swing."

Boris filled up Pamela's glass. "Do you like golf, Pamela?" he asked.

Pamela felt an odd sensation on her lips. It was something she hadn't felt for a very long time. Then she laughed, too. "I hate golf," she said. "It's really, really, really boring."

"Pamela!" gasped Dudley. "You never told me that!"

Laughter shook Pamela's body. "You never asked!"

It turned out that Anaconda was a complete natural at golf.

She could hit a ball perfectly every time.
"You really must join the golf club," said
Dudley.

Meanwhile, Boris and Pamela were
discussing garden design.

Gardening was a great hobby of Boris's, but the idea of putting flowers into beds had never occurred to him.

Ruby, Pearl, Clod, and Simon had run off as soon as their parents had finished drinking the rainbow punch.

Everything was going beautifully.

That is, until they heard the *smash!* of breaking glass.

They stared down at the floor.

A large rock wrapped in paper lay in a pile of broken glass at their feet. Nobody spoke. Boris bent down and picked up the paper.

Words were written across the paper in black, ugly letters:

GET OUT OR YOUR
HOUSE BURNS DOWN.
YOU HAVE BEEN WARNED.

CHAPTER 9

"Almost finished," said Simon from underneath the strange airplane.

The plane's body was made out of car panels, painted silver with a red stripe along its side. The wings were two thin lengths of wood covered in stretched canvas. The engine, which came out of an old sports car, was fixed to the front and attached to a rod that turned the propeller. Clod thought it was the most beautiful thing he had ever seen.

"One more turn." Simon picked up a large wrench and yanked it hard. Then he stood up and grinned. "Let's give it a try!"

Clod could hardly breathe, he was so excited. "Wait till they see us! Wait till they see us!" He had brought a special camera so he could take a picture of everyone's amazed faces. Clod let out a huge whoop of delight. "They'll never believe it!"

The two boys pushed the plane to the end of garden where there was a gap in the hedge. On the other side of the hedge was a long field where the grass was smooth enough for the plane to take off.

"Ready?" Simon climbed into the pilot's seat, strapped on his seat-belt, and put on a pair of goggles.

"Ready," shouted Clod. He jumped in and pulled on a pair of ski goggles.

They both wore woolly hats, ski mitts, and long, warm scarves wrapped around their necks.

Simon crossed his fingers, then turned the key of the old sports car engine. It started! In front of them the blades of the plane's propeller slowly started to turn.

"It works! It works!" shouted Simon.

"Yee-haw!" yelled Clod, punching his fist into the air.

The blades whirled around and around. When they were just a blur, Simon moved the joystick forward. There was a bump and the plane began to move. A moment later they were racing across the grass. Faster and faster! Suddenly the plane shuddered and the ground beneath them disappeared!

They were flying!

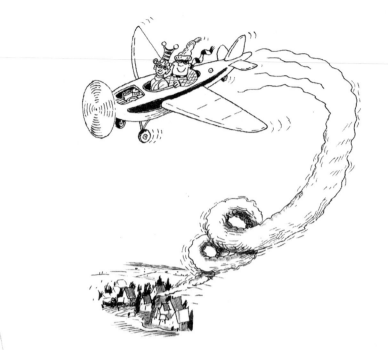

Clod felt the wind roar past his face as they climbed high over the treetops. The noise of the wind and the engine was so loud it was impossible to talk.

They flew above Primrose Drive, and turned to swoop over their parents' party.

In the setting sun, the towers of No. 34 Primrose Drive glowed gold and red. It looked like a castle surrounded by a thick, green jungle.

Suddenly something else glittered gold!

Clod and Simon looked across to No. 33. It was Goldie Bouncer's yellow hair! Clod and Simon watched as she climbed out of a window and ran after a man holding a briefcase.

It was Sid Bouncer. In front of him, a red car was waiting in the road. Simon thought he was going to be sick. He remembered what Ruby told him she had seen in the safe. "Nothing but a boring old briefcase," she'd said.

Simon knew it wasn't just any briefcase. It was the briefcase Dudley had taken with him when he had gone to the bank. In that split second, Simon knew that Sid was stealing his father's money!

Even though Clod didn't know about the money in the briefcase, he could see that someone was stealing something from Simon's parents.

As fast as he could, he pulled out his camera and took a picture.

Then he wrote three words on a tiny notepad and showed it to Simon:

Follow the car.

Simon turned a wide circle as fast as he could at a safe distance, so that Sid and Goldie wouldn't suspect anything.

The little plane followed the red car as it drove through the streets and headed out of town. At last the red car stopped in front of a tiny trailer next to a used-car lot.

Clod scribbled another note:

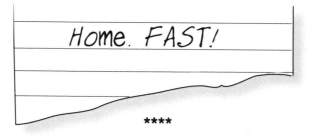

Home. FAST!

****

The moment Pamela saw the smashed window and the rock, she knew she and Dudley had made a terrible mistake.

She sat on the floor with her head in her hands. "I'm so sorry," she sobbed. "I never thought Sid Bouncer would do something so horrible!"

A huge sigh passed through Pamela's body. "Oh, Dudley. We've been so selfish and unkind."

She turned to Anaconda.

"Will you ever forgive us?" Then Pamela explained about the plan that Sid Bouncer and her husband had made about the Wolfbane home.

"It's our fault, too," Anaconda said. "We didn't know our changes would upset the neighbors. But it's wonderful that our children get along so well. Pearl and Clod have never had real friends before."

Pamela looked up through teary eyes. "Neither have Ruby and Simon."

"That settles it then," said Anaconda. "The children must not be upset."

Boris grabbed a lighter, picked up the paper that had been wrapped around the rock, and set fire to it.

Boris stamped out the burned pieces that fluttered to the floor. "Let's forget all about it," he said. "It's over now."

"I hope so," replied Dudley.

At that moment, Pearl, Ruby, Clod, and Simon rushed into the room. Their faces were white and frightened. "Something awful happened!" cried Simon.

"Sid Bouncer stole the briefcase from your safe!" cried Ruby.

Dudley rubbed his hands over his face. He felt as if he was falling down a cliff.

"Are you sure?" asked Boris.

Clod nodded. "I even took a picture of them from the airplane we built." He looked at his mother. "That was the surprise we were making."

Pamela turned to Simon as if she was in a dream. Her eyes were big and round. "You were flying an airplane?" she whispered. For the second time that day, Pamela sank to the floor.

CHAPTER 10

"My life's savings," cried Dudley as he stared at the safe. "He's stolen my life's savings!" Dudley slumped down on a chair. On the other side of the room, the gold grate was open. The safe was empty.

"Don't worry, Dudley dear," said Anaconda. "We"ll steal it back and everything will be normal again."

"Normal!" cried Pamela. "It was that stupid idea that got us into all this mess in the first place."

Ruby was so surprised her eyes almost popped out. "But you want everyone to be normal," she almost shouted.

Pamela looked at her daughter. "Everyone makes mistakes," she said.

Ruby couldn't believe what she was hearing. "So you won't try to make me wear pretty, pink clothes anymore?"

"No more pretty, pink clothes," replied her mother in a hollow voice.

Ruby narrowed her eyes. "So I can give them to Pearl?"

"Ruby!" said Pearl. "I can't take those!"

"Oh, yes you can," cried Ruby. "I'll trade them for the ones you don't like that your mother keeps giving you!"

Anaconda looked at Pearl. "You mean the old, black, velvet ones? I thought you liked the old, black, velvet ones," she said.

Pearl rolled her eyes. "Mom," she said in a patient voice. "You think I like the torn gray ones and the designer ripped purple ones."

"Wow!" cried Ruby. "I never thought I'd get excited about clothes!" Everyone began to laugh.

"Excuse me, ladies," said Boris firmly. "Perhaps you can talk about clothes another time? We have more serious things to think about now."

He turned to Dudley. "Where does this Sid Bouncer live?"

"One of those big houses by the golf course," replied Dudley.

"No, he doesn't," said Simon. "He lives in a trailer next to a used-car lot."

"We followed him in the airplane!" cried Clod.

Anaconda's eyes lit up. A plan was taking shape in her head. "Why don't Clod and Simon keep watch from their airplane while the rest of us go by car?" she said.

"But what if the Bouncers escape?" asked Pearl. "How will we know?"

"My walkie-talkies!" shouted Clod suddenly. "We'll have one and you'll have the other." He rushed out the door.

"Good idea, Clod," cried Simon.

The tiniest spark of hope flickered in Dudley's eyes. "We could all fit in my car," he said.

Simon shook his head. "I forgot to tell you. The tires are all flat. They let the air out."

"Then we'll go in our carriage," cried Boris. "The horses could use a good gallop!"

Ten minutes later, Dudley was sitting beside Boris in the strangest carriage he had ever seen. It was black with spidery wheels covered with green scum. Inside, Pearl, Ruby, Anaconda, and Pamela hadn't stopped talking from the moment they sat down on the velvet seats.

Dudley was amazed. Even though everything seemed to be going wrong, he was almost enjoying himself.

As the carriage turned out of Primrose Drive, there was a roar overhead.

A strange airplane shot across the sky. Simon and Clod waved. Then the plane turned and headed across the town.

"Your boy's a genius," shouted Boris above the noise of the hooves. "You must be very proud of him."

Dudley *was* proud of Simon, even though he had never been able to show it. "I am proud of him," shouted Dudley. "And he and Clod make a great team!"

"Excellent!" shouted Boris in reply. He shook the reins and the horses shot forward onto the main road.

As trees and houses flashed past, Dudley thought about what had happened. He couldn't believe he had been so selfish.

It was because he had been frightened. Frightened to appear different. Frightened not to fit in. And that had made him into someone who was mean and greedy.

"Silver Bird to Stagecoach! Silver Bird to Stagecoach!" The walkie-talkie in Dudley's hand crackled into life.

Dudley was so surprised he nearly fell off the seat. "Come in, Silver Bird!"

"They're gone!" Clod's voice shouted. "We've looked for them everywhere! What should we do?"

Boris held out his hand for the walkie-talkie. "Land and wait for us," he shouted. "We're almost there."

Then to Dudley's amazement, a great grin spread across Boris's face. "Don't give up," he cried. "Anaconda's got a nose like a bloodhound. They won't get far!"

CHAPTER 11

The tiny trailer looked like a hurricane had gone through it. There were bills and old clothes tossed all over the place.

While the children took turns flying in the airplane, the adults crammed into the trailer and sat on the cramped seats.

Anaconda examined everything.

Pamela stared as Anaconda searched through hundreds of hotel brochures that were scattered on the floor.

They came from all over the world and they were all very fancy. Suddenly she pounced on one.

"Got them!" Anaconda cried. "They're flying to Spain tomorrow."

Neither Dudley nor Pamela said anything. There was nothing to say. They were too late.

Their life savings were gone. Sid and Goldie had escaped.

"We're not too late!" said Anaconda. "There's a reservation for a room at the Regency Ritz Hotel tonight! We'll put on our best clothes and trap them!"

* * *

Simon and Clod didn't care what clothes they wore to the Regency Ritz. Nobody else minded, either, as long as they wiped the grease off their faces.

Ruby looked sensational in Pearl's shredded black skirt and black top.

Pearl looked stunning in Ruby's lacy, silver party dress with blue shoes.

Boris was delighted. "You both look absolutely lovely," he cried.

"Splendid!" said Dudley.

Anaconda wanted to pop open a bottle of champagne then and there.

But Boris said no. They were running out of time already and they still had to make two stops on the way to the hotel.

One was a camera film store called "Develop on the Spot."

The other was the police station.

* * *

At the Regency Ritz Hotel, Sid lifted a glass bubbling with champagne.

Goldie picked up her glass and twisted her arm through his. What a great team they made!

"To us," said Sid.

"To us," replied Goldie. She smiled and winked at Sid.

They clinked their glasses together.

Then, as if pulled by some strange force, they both looked in the same direction.

The Rigid-Smythes and the Wolfbanes were all walking, together, into the hotel's dining room!

Goldie sprayed her dainty sip of champagne all over the place.

Sid's hand stayed frozen in midair.

Goldie stared as the two families settled themselves around a big table.

"Sid," hissed Goldie. "I don't know what's going on and I don't want to know. But we've got to get out of here fast."

Sid's eyes snapped open twice but he still couldn't move.

"Sid!" hissed Goldie again.

"I'm thinking!" he said.

Behind them a pair of glass doors led out to a patio.

"We'll go through those doors and around the side of the hotel," Sid said quickly. "Then you go and pack, and meet me in the lobby. I'll get the briefcase out of the hotel safe."

CHAPTER 12

Ruby leaned over and nudged Pearl in the ribs. Her eyes sparkled like black pearls. "Who would have thought it?" she whispered with a huge grin on her face.

Pearl knew exactly what she meant. Across the table Pamela and Anaconda were laughing and talking.

"You must tell me where you do your shopping," said Anaconda. "It's Pearl's birthday soon and I'd love to get it right, if you know what I mean."

"I know exactly what you mean," replied Pamela. "I've gotten it wrong too, for so long!"

"Any minute now," said Boris, looking at his watch.

Dudley swallowed nervously.

The sergeant at the police station had been very interested in the photograph and their story when the families had stopped on their way to the Regency Ritz.

The police had been following the careers of Sid and Goldie Bouncer for years. The problem, the sergeant said, was that they had never been able to get enough evidence to put them in jail.

Dudley was shocked. "You mean Sid's done this sort of thing before?"

"Yes!" replied the sergeant. "You'd be surprised how many people fall for it."

He shook his head. "It's exactly the same scam every time. The only things that ever change are Sid's name and the color of Goldie's hair."

So the police sergeant, Dudley, and Boris worked out a plan that would trap Sid and Goldie but not spoil the children's fun and everyone else's evening out.

All that Dudley had to do was identify his briefcase in the hotel safe, and the moment Sid tried to collect it, he and Goldie would be arrested.

"But how will we know when they're gone?" Dudley had asked nervously.

The policeman had laughed.

"We'll send in a big bottle of champagne," he told Boris.

"Excellent," said Boris, smiling.

* * *

Later, Dudley looked at his watch again. It was only a minute since he had checked it, but the seconds felt like hours.

"Free champagne," said a voice.

A waiter put an enormous silver bucket on the table. Inside it was a giant bottle of champagne!

It was the moment Dudley had been waiting for!

Sid and Goldie Bouncer would not be cheating anybody else again for a long, long time!

Across the table, Pearl and Ruby saw their parents exchange the strangest looks. Both girls could sense a huge feeling of relief and happiness.

Even though they didn't know what Sid and Goldie had been planning, they knew something very important had happened.

Things were going to be different for them all from now on.

There was a huge *pop!* as the waiter opened the champagne and quickly filled everyone's glass.

"I would like to propose a toast," said Boris Wolfbane. He stood up and smiled. "To friends and neighbors!"

Dudley Rigid Smythe turned bright red. Then he stood up beside Boris.

"To friends and neighbors," he cried.

Even though it was the fanciest hotel in town, Anaconda and Pamela, Ruby and Pearl, and Clod and Simon all jumped up and let out the loudest cheer they could.

In that moment, Pearl realized that it didn't matter if people lived different lives.

It didn't matter if Anaconda and Boris had a mud hole or if the Rigid-Smythes had a sparkling blue swimming pool.

Pearl and Ruby turned to each other at the same time. It was as if they were both thinking the same thing.

"You're my best friend," said Ruby.

"You're my best friend, too," whispered Pearl. She smiled.

While the others were laughing and cheering, Pearl and Ruby wrapped their arms around each other and hugged as hard as they could.

About the Author

Karen Wallace is the author of more than one hundred books for children, and the winner of several book awards. She was born in Canada and grew up in a log cabin in the woods of Quebec. She has also lived in France and Ireland, and has worked making pizzas, and singing in a cabaret and a bluegrass band. Writing is her favorite activity. Wallace says she has spent most of her life making up stories.

Glossary

anaconda (an-uh-KON-duh)—a very long snake that lives in South America

comfy (KUM-fee)—comfortable

crave (KRAVE)—to desire or want

evidence (EV-uh-denss)—proof that something happened

genius (JEEN-yuss)—someone who has a great talent to think or to make things

grate (GRATE)—a frame of crossed metal bars that might cover a window or opening

greed (GREED)—a selfish desire to want more and more of something

gumption (GUMP-shun)—courage

scam (SKAM)—a sneaky plan to cheat someone out of their money or belongings

Discussion Questions

1. What makes people different from one another? Why do you think people are frightened of people who are different from them? What can they do about it?

2. The author calls the book *Something Slimy on Primrose Drive*. Is that a good title? What is slimy? Is it the Wolfbane's house, or is it Sid's sneaky plan?

3. Have you ever felt nervous or scared about fitting in with a new group of people or trying to make new friends? What did you do? How did you feel?

Writing Prompts

1. What do you think is important about life? Is it different from what your parents think is important, or is it the same? Write a paragraph and tell us.

2. The characters in the book have very special names. Make a list of the characters and explain how you think the names seem to fit each person.

3. Boris and Anaconda think their house is cozy and comfortable. Most people would think it is not! Describe your own perfect house. Tell us what kind of bedroom you would make for yourself.

Also by
Karen Wallace

Aargh, It's an Alien!

*Albert's parents give him everything
he wants, except time with them.
Can the aliens find a way to make
Albert's life more fun?*

Also Published by Stone Arch Books

James and the Alien Experiment
by S. Prue

When James is abducted by aliens, he undergoes some drastic changes. His new super strength, super brains, and super speed, however, bring more problems than James bargained for.

Time and Again
by Rob Childs

Becky and Chris discover a strange-looking watch with the power to travel back through time. Time travel is not as easy as they thought, especially when the class troublemaker, Luke, decides to join them.

Internet Sites

Do you want to know more about subjects related to this book? Or are you interested in learning about other topics? Then check out FactHound, a fun, easy way to find Internet sites.

Our investigative staff has already sniffed out great sites for you!

Here's how to use FactHound:

1. Visit *www.facthound.com*

2. Select your grade level.

3. To learn more about subjects related to this book, type in the book's ISBN number: **1598891138**.

4. Click the **Fetch It** button.

FactHound will fetch the best Internet sites for you!